This book is dedicated to Mr. Parkin (and his sisters) and Mr. Pancake.

This book positively belongs to:

Paulina P.
(for Petersen)

by Lisa Cinar

Simply Read Books

Paulina P. (for Petersen)
loves the letter P, indeederson.
If a thing starts with a P,
Paulina loves it instantly!

Pencils, pennies, ping pong, pickles,
animals that sometimes prickle,
parmesan, pajamas, plants,
polka-dotted underpants,
polyester pantyhose,
popsicles (a pair of those),
paisley patterns, poetry,
name anything that starts with P,
Paulina loves it—
INSTANTLY!

If perchance Paulina sees
a thing that DOESN'T start with P,
oh how she will sniff and sneer,
like she does at these things here:

#1 Anything
heart-shaped

I made you
a card!

Out of all the
things you can
draw! Hearts?
Pfft! Please!

#2 Yellow frilly dresses

Preposterous!

#3 Chocolate bar at the movies

But you can get popcorn!!!
So many Ps in one bag!

#4 Color by numbers

Perplexing!

Now you're asking, "Tell me why?!"
To which simply I reply,
she just prefers the letter P.
Read along and you will see…

Sometimes when Paulina plays,
she's a pirate on rough waves
or a panda running wild,
not her mother's perfect child!

Paulina! What are you
doing to my plant?!

I am not Paulina!
I am a panda!

Sometimes she's a pharmacist
and has a long prescription list.

A pony pendant is for you
if you are feeling oh so blue.
A paper mask is quick to send
unwanted monsters to their end.
A party hat will make you smile
and sing and dance in party style.
A pinecone can repel a liar.
Or try a piece of dragon phyre.

P is so perfect it takes two
to do all the P things she likes to do.
Paulina's pal is Penny Lee,
who plays along with the letter P.

They piggyback, plan picnic trips,
and hop around on pogo-sticks.
They pose and plot and poke like pokers—
a real couple of practical jokers!

plrhplrh...

pfffffhht...

they paint their portraits, some with frames.

When I grow up, I'm sure you'll guess,
I want to be a painter, yes!
My early work, as you will see
revolves around the letter P!

Here are some of my precious paintings:

Polite Penguins in a Predicament

Very nice, Paulina... BUT the assignment was to paint a zebra!

But zebra doesn't start with P!

Paulina's Art teacher

Pointy Pencil
in the Park

Paulina's Math teacher

Yes, it's a great painting, Paulina... BUT where are problems 8 to 24?!

Extra credit perhaps?

Polar Bear with Popsicle

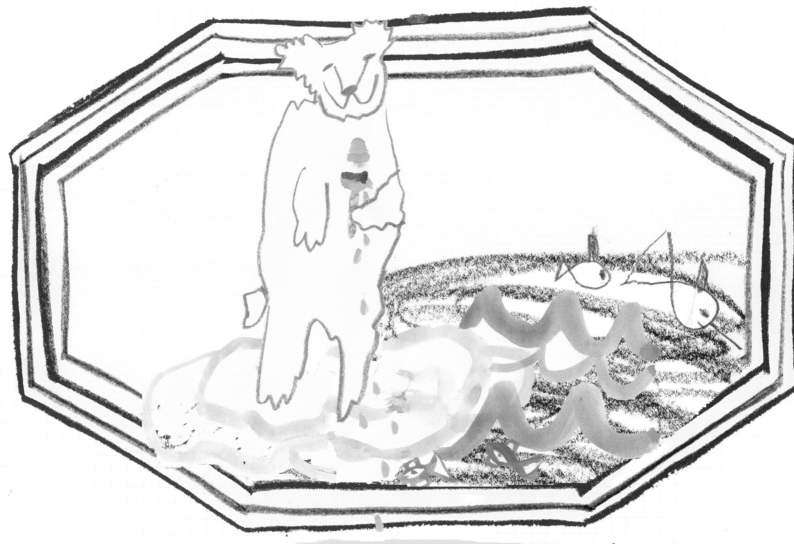

Penny

I love it!!! Could you paint me a polar bear just like that?! BUT ... holding a HEART instead of a popsicle?

A heart?! Pha! Preposterous! Hearts have nothing to do with the letter P!

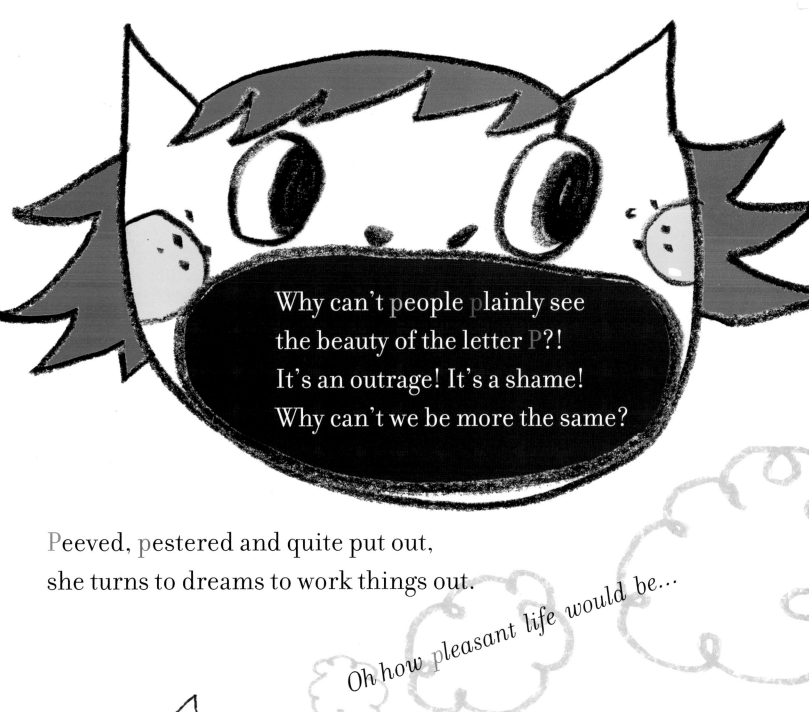

Why can't people plainly see
the beauty of the letter P?!
It's an outrage! It's a shame!
Why can't we be more the same?

Peeved, pestered and quite put out,
she turns to dreams to work things out.

Oh how pleasant life would be...

… if everyone became… a pea!

How peaceful.

Even worse, how would it be to HAVE to be like *Penny Lee!*

I'll never stop being true to me!

MY favorite thing is the letter P!

And it's HEARTS for Penny Lee!

Our differences suit us... PERFECTLY!

The End

FOR PENNY

FROM: PAULINA

Paulina would also especially like to thank Penny Lee (aka Kallie George) and Tiffany Stone for partaking in this passionate plight.

First published in 2009 by Simply Read Books
www.simplyreadbooks.com

Text & Illustrations © 2009 Lisa Cinar

Library and Archives Canada Cataloguing in Publication

Cinar, Lisa, 1980-
          Paulina P. (for Petersen) / Lisa Cinar.

Interest age level: For ages 3-7.
ISBN 978-1-897476-09-3

          I. Title.

PS8605.I53 P38 2009   jC813'.6   C2009-900801-7

We gratefully acknowledge the support of the Canada Council for the Arts, the Government of Canada through the Book Publishing Industry Development Program and the BC Arts Council for our publishing program.

Book Design by Steedman Design

Printed in Singapore

10 9 8 7 6 5 4 3 2 1